D0323517

Power Play

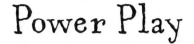

Twink

Bimi

Pix

Sooze

Sili

Mariella

Kiki

Ivy

Glitterwings Academy

Book Thirteen

Power Play

Titania Woods
Illustrated by Smiljana Coh

BLOOMSBURY
LONDON BERLIN NEW YORK

Bloomsbury Publishing, London, Berlin and New York

First published in Great Britain in April 2010 by Bloomsbury Publishing Plc
36 Soho Square, London, W1D 3QY

A CIP catalogue record of this book is available from the British Library

ISBN 978 1 4088 0269 4

All papers used by Bloomsbury Publishing are natural, recyclable products made
from wood grown in well-managed forests. The manufacturing processes conform to
the environmental regulations of the country of origin.

Typeset by Dorchester Typesetting Group Ltd
Printed in Singapore by Tien Wah Press

1 3 5 7 9 10 8 6 4 2

www.glitterwingsacademy.co.uk

To Linda C., a glimmery friend

Chapter One

Twink Flutterby felt very grown-up as she and her younger sister Teena flew through the bright spring afternoon. For the first time, their parents were allowing her and Teena to fly to Glitterwings Academy on their own. Twink was a fourth-year student now, and they knew they could trust her to be sensible.

Her fourth year at Glitterwings! Twink shook her head in wonder. It hardly seemed possible that she'd been attending the famous fairy school for so long.

'Oof! I liked it better when Dad flew with us,' moaned Teena. She was flying along slowly, weighed down by her oak-leaf bag. With her long pink hair and lavender wings, Teena looked a lot like her older sister – apart from her expression, which was very cross at the moment!

Twink grinned as she swooped to avoid a yellow butterfly flitting past. 'We're almost there,' she said. 'Look, there's the hill!'

The two sisters skimmed over the grassy slope and Glitterwings Academy came into view: a massive oak tree with tiny golden windows spiralling up its trunk. At its base sat a pair of grand double doors, open in welcome. Returning fairies hovered about the tree in rainbow clusters, laughing and chatting.

Twink sighed happily as she and Teena touched down on the front lawn. It was glimmery to be back – especially in the springtime, which meant a new Fledge season! Twink had been a member of the school Fledge team since her second year, and her wings tingled at the thought of playing the high-speed game again.

'There's Zuzu,' said Teena, spotting her best friend. 'See you later, Twink!' She sped off towards the second-year section.

Twink smiled as she caught sight of her own best friend, Bimi Bluebell. She was standing beside a tree root, talking to a fairy called Kiki. Grabbing up her oak-leaf bag, Twink skimmed around the tree root and landed at her side. 'Hi, Bimi!'

'Twink!' Bimi spun towards her. 'Hurrah, you're here!'

The two friends hugged, bouncing up and down. Bimi had long, midnight-blue hair, and silver wings with golden swirls on them. Though easily the prettiest fairy in the school, she was very down-to-earth and not vain in the least.

'Hi, Kiki,' said Twink as she and Bimi separated. 'Did you have good hols?' It was strange to think how jealous she'd been of Kiki when the violet-haired fairy first arrived at Glitterwings – now she thought she was one of the nicest fairies in their year.

'Glimmery!' said Kiki. 'Have you checked in yet? We were just about to.'

The three fairies flew over to the fourth-year check-in area together, chattering about their hols. The fourth-year head was Miss Petal, their Flower Power teacher, and she greeted them warmly.

'Welcome back, girls,' she said, ticking them off her clover-leaf list. 'You're all in Bluebell Branch this year.'

Twink nudged Bimi with her wing. 'That's perfect for *you*, isn't it?' she teased.

'Bimi Bluebell in Bluebell Branch!' giggled Bimi. 'Yes, that sounds about right. Shall we go up and have a look?'

'You two go ahead; I'm going to see if Ivy has got here yet,' said Kiki. Ivy was Kiki's best friend, a green-haired fairy as artistic as she was.

'OK – we'll see you up at Bluebell Branch!' called Twink over her shoulder as she and Bimi flew off. Skimming through the arched double doors together, the two friends swooped into the school.

As always, Twink found herself smiling as she took in her surroundings. The inside of Glitterwings Academy was a tall, golden tower, filled with light. For as high as the eye could see, fairies darted in and out of the tree's branches like brightly coloured birds.

Twink and Bimi spiralled quickly upwards, passing sleeping branches and classrooms filled with red-spotted mushroom seats. 'I'm going to miss Violet Branch,' said Twink wistfully as they passed their branch from the year before. 'Wasn't it glimmery, having our beds up in loft spaces?'

Bimi nodded. 'But maybe Bluebell Branch will be nice, too.'

'There it is!' said Twink, spotting a cluster of

bright blue flowers hanging over a ledge. With a flutter of wings, she and Bimi landed and pushed open the door.

'Oh!' gasped Twink.

Bimi was right. If anything, their new room was even nicer than Violet Branch! It was located in a section of bough that grew straight up, like a tower of its own. Up above, two round loft spaces encircled the walls, one over the other, each with four mossy beds. A large bunch of bluebells hung from the centre of the ceiling like a flowered chandelier.

Several of their friends had already arrived, and a chorus of voices greeted them. 'Hello, Opposite!' called a fairy, flying down from the higher loft space to scoop Twink into a hug.

'Hi, Sooze,' said Twink happily, returning the embrace. Sooze had lavender hair and pink wings – the exact *opposite* of Twink. The two had been best friends once, and were still close.

'Oh, isn't this pretty!' exclaimed Bimi, looking around her. 'Sooze, can Twink and I join you up top?'

Sooze grinned and lowered her voice. 'You can if you want – but Mariella's up there, too.'

Twink and Bimi glanced at each other, and wrinkled their noses in unison. 'Maybe we'll take the bottom loft instead,' said Twink. Though Mariella had improved greatly in the three years since they'd known her, the pointy-faced fairy could still be very irritating – though oddly enough, she and Sooze seemed to get on all right now!

Flying to the lower loft space, Bimi and Twink took mossy beds side by side. Each had a cluster of bluebells hanging over it, with a window to one side – and because of the round walls, each window had a different view.

To Twink's delight, she could see the school Fledge field from hers, just visible far below. Soon she'd be playing with the team again – she could hardly wait! Then Twink frowned thoughtfully. Who would their new Games Fairy be, now that Madge was gone?

'Let me guess, Twink – you're looking forward to Fledge starting up!' said a clever fairy called Pix,

who had one of the other beds in their loft.

Twink turned away from the window with a sheepish grin. 'Is it that obvious?'

A silvery-haired fairy called Sili had taken the other bed, and the four of them chatted as they unpacked their things. 'Oh, isn't it lovely to be Fourth Years!' exclaimed Sili, fluttering her wings with a rapturous sigh.

With an impish expression, Pix tucked a strand of red hair behind a pointed ear. 'Yes, and you know what *that* means – we get to make our own uniforms tomorrow!'

'I wonder what Sooze's will be like,' said Bimi, placing a bottle of wing polish on her bedside mushroom.

Twink giggled, imagining it. Sooze could be very mischievous at times, and would probably enjoy horrifying their matron, Mrs Hover, with some wild creation!

Ivy and Kiki arrived, taking the last two beds in the upper loft space, and soon afterwards it was time for the opening session. The Bluebell Branch fairies

flew down together, joining long streams of other fairies as everyone headed towards the Great Branch. Twink smiled to see the First Years riding on their birds. They looked completely terrified!

The Great Branch was the largest branch in the school, with arched windows and gleaming wooden floors. The long room was filled with rows of mossy tables, each with a different flower dangling over it, so that the Branch was like a sunny springtime garden.

The Bluebell Branch table was over to one side. Twink perched on a spotted mushroom beside Bimi. Glancing around, she spotted Teena at the Daisy Branch table, and the two sisters exchanged a wave.

'Good afternoon, girls!' said a deep voice from the front of the Branch. Silence fell as the students turned to face Miss Shimmery, their HeadFairy. The stately white-haired fairy hovered above a platform at the front of the branch, her rainbow wings gleaming like opals.

'I hope you had a lovely holiday – and a very warm welcome to all our new students!' Miss

Shimmery beamed down at the first-year tables, who managed nervous smiles in return. 'Now, I have just a few announcements . . .'

Twink settled back on to her mushroom seat as Miss Shimmery went on: school uniforms would be required from tomorrow; there was to be no high-speed flying in the trunk, no bothering the water sprites who lived in the school pond . . . Twink thought with amusement that she could probably have given the talk herself. She practically knew it by heart now!

Miss Shimmery adjusted her sparkle specs with a twinkle in her eyes. 'And as for our first-year students, Mrs Lightwing will sprinkle you with fairy dust immediately after breakfast tomorrow, so that you can have your first flying lesson.'

Excited whispers broke out among the First Years. The rest of the school grinned, remembering the wonder of flying for the very first time.

Miss Shimmery glanced down at her petal pad. 'Finally, there will be a meeting of the school Fledge team here in the Great Branch tonight after dinner

– you have a lot to decide, as I'm sure you're aware. And now, I think it's time for our meal. Butterflies commence!'

Raising her arm in the air, Miss Shimmery drifted back down to the platform. The double doors to the Great Branch swung open, and a bright stream of butterflies bobbed in, each carrying a tray of seed cakes or a pitcher of fresh morning dew.

'What does the Fledge team have to decide?' asked Bimi as a purple butterfly placed a tray of seed cakes on their table.

'We have to elect a new Games Fairy,' explained Twink. Madge had completed her sixth year at Glitterwings the term before, leaving the team leaderless.

Bimi's blue eyes grew round. 'Oh! Who do you think it'll be?'

Twink shrugged, reaching for a seed cake. 'Well, it's Cassi and Zayna's first year on the team; they were both reserve players last year. So I suppose it'll have to be either Vera or Romi.'

She frowned slightly at the thought. Though Vera was a good player, she was lazy – and Romi, while an excellent player, could be difficult to get on with. Neither choice was really ideal, but Twink didn't see who else it could be.

'*You* should do it, Opposite,' put in Sooze from across the table. 'You'd be better than either of those two moss brains!'

'Me?' Twink's voice came out in a squeak. 'Don't be daft, Sooze – I'm only a fourth-year student.'

Pix had been listening as well, and she shrugged as she helped herself to a seed cake. 'Well, Madge was

only a Fourth Year when she started as Games Fairy.'

Twink realised in surprise that she was right. 'Yes, but –' She stopped, and shook her head. 'Honestly, this is silly! It's up to the team, not me.'

'Well, I know who *I'd* vote for,' said Bimi firmly. 'I think they're right, Twink. It should be you, not Vera or Romi.'

'I'm not listening any more,' laughed Twink. 'Now come on, everyone, let's change the subject.'

But as the conversation moved on to other things, Twink found her thoughts returning to who would be the new Games Fairy. It was ridiculous, of course – why would the team vote for her, instead of one of the older girls? Even so, Twink found herself drifting into an exciting daydream with herself as the new team leader.

Now stop it, she scolded herself as she poured fresh dew into her acorn cup. *It's up to the team, and that's that!*

Chapter Two

After dinner, the Fledge team remained behind once the Great Branch had emptied, sitting together at the Lilac Branch table. Miss Shimmery took a seat with them, folding her rainbow wings neatly behind her back.

'I'm sure you all know what this meeting is about,' she said. 'Does anyone have any thoughts as to which of you should be the new Games Fairy?'

Twink and the others glanced at each other. Though a Fledge team normally had eight members – six players plus two reserves – there were only five

of them present. Several team members had left along with Madge the previous term, including a fairy called Mia, who had moved away. It was a shame, thought Twink. Mia would have been the perfect Games Fairy!

'Well?' prompted Miss Shimmery after a moment.

Romi, a fifth-year fairy with short purple hair, looked like she wanted to say something, but didn't. Suddenly Twink realised that Vera was gazing at her with a speculative smile. All at once the older fairy raised her hand.

'Yes, Vera? Do you have any ideas?' asked Miss Shimmery.

Vera nodded. She was a sixth-year student with long golden hair, and now she flipped it back confidently as she addressed the others. 'Yes. I nominate Twink!'

Twink's jaw dropped open. '*Me?*' she gasped. 'But I'm only a Fourth Year! Why not you, Vera?'

She knew the moment she said it that Vera would never agree. Though she was wonderful on the Fledge field, Vera was always moaning about having to work too hard, and had complained about

Madge's strictness whenever the Games Fairy's back had been turned. Being the Games Fairy herself was the last thing she'd want to do!

Sure enough, Vera shook her head. 'No, I want to enjoy myself on the Fledge field this year, not take on more work! Besides, it's better for it to be a younger student, so that you'll have the team for several years instead of only one.'

Twink's heart began to thud as she realised Vera was right. She looked around the table. 'Well . . . what do the rest of you think?'

'I think *I* should be the Games Fairy, not you!' burst out Romi. Her cheeks flushed as she glanced guiltily at Miss Shimmery. The HeadFairy made no comment. 'I nominate myself,' went on Romi. 'No offence, Twink, but I'm a better player than you.'

'I never said you weren't,' protested Twink, stung. 'I know you are – you're bigger and stronger than me.'

Zayna, who was Vera's best friend on the team, leaned forward. 'No, be fair, Romi – you're a better Guard, but not a better Stealer. Twink's the best of any of us at that.'

Cassi, a fifth-year fairy with white wings, nodded. 'And besides, being the Games Fairy isn't about who plays the best, it's about who can *lead* us the best – isn't it, Miss Shimmery?'

'Indeed,' said Miss Shimmery. She smiled at them over her sparkle specs. 'Well, so far we have two nominations to consider: Romi and Twink. Would anyone like to put another name forward?'

Silence fell. Romi frowned, tapping her wings together.

'Very well, the vote for the new Games Fairy will be between those two,' said Miss Shimmery. She

handed out pieces of rose petal, along with some snail-trail pens. 'Please write down your choice, and then fold your petal over and pass it back to me,' she instructed.

Twink's mouth felt dry as she uncapped her pen. Hardly daring to breathe, she quickly scribbled down her own name, and then folded the petal tightly and handed it to Miss Shimmery.

Once all five petals had been returned to her, Miss Shimmery carefully unfolded each one, reading it silently. Twink's pulse pounded as she watched. Had the others voted for Romi after all? She could hardly blame them if they had – Romi really *was* the better player, no matter what Zayna had said.

But after she had opened all five petals, Miss Shimmery smiled warmly at her. 'Congratulations, Twink – you're the new Games Fairy! Would you like to say a few words?'

Feeling as if she were in a dream, Twink stood up. The rest of the team was beaming at her – apart from Romi, whose mouth was in a tight line.

'Um . . . thank you!' stammered Twink, gripping

the edge of the table. 'I never expected this, I really didn't. I'll do the best job I can for you, I promise!'

'You'll be brilliant!' said Vera with a grin. 'Come on, everyone – three cheers for our new Games Fairy.'

The team clapped their wings together as they loudly *hip-hip-hooray*ed her. Romi joined in with the others, though it was clear her heart wasn't in it. Twink felt her cheeks turn pink.

'Well done, girls,' said Miss Shimmery, rising from her seat. 'And Twink, I'm sure that you'll want to have try-outs soon for the open place on the team, plus the two reserve positions. Post a notice whenever you're ready.'

'Yes, I'll – I'll do it before I go to bed tonight,' said Twink in a daze.

Romi stopped her as the team flitted from the Great Branch. 'Well, I suppose the best fairy won,' she said, offering her wing to Twink. 'I still think I'd have been a better Games Fairy, but I'll give you all the help I can.' *Because you're going to need it*, her expression seemed to say.

'Thanks,' said Twink drily, touching her wing to

Romi's. But she was too happy to be really irritated. She wasn't quite sure how it had happened – but *she* was the new Games Fairy! She really was!

The thrill still hadn't worn off by the next morning, when the school birds delivered a pile of fresh blue-bell blossoms to the Bluebell Branch ledge. Twink chose one dreamily for her new uniform, hardly paying attention as she used a pinch of fairy dust to transform it into a dress.

Bimi burst out laughing at the sight of it. 'Oi, Games Fairy – do you really plan to wear that?'

Twink looked down in surprise, and saw that she had used the green stalk of the bluebell instead of the flower! She giggled as she changed the dress back. 'No, I suppose not.'

Trying again, Twink paid more attention this time and created a pretty dress with a plain blue bodice and sleeves, and a skirt made of tiny bluebell blossoms.

'That's more like it,' said Bimi, wearing a similar frock.

'Ta-da!' called Sooze from the upper loft space.

Arms out, she drifted down to the ground. The branch caught its breath at the sight of her, and then exploded into howls of hilarity.

'Sooze! You can't wear *that*,' squealed Mariella, peering over the edge of their loft for a better look.

'Why not?' said Sooze. Fluttering her wings, she struck a pose. 'It's a dress made of bluebells, isn't it?'

'Barely!' laughed Pix.

Twink grinned as she took it in. Sooze's skirt had a long slit up one side, and layers of cascading flounces on the other. One sleeve was long and tight, the other sleeve was missing altogether – and around Sooze's neck was draped a long feathery boa of bluebells! She twirled it in one hand as she grinned at them.

'You're all just jealous. It's a *great* dress, isn't it, Kiki?' The violet-haired fairy's mother was a fashion designer, and Kiki herself was very skilled at dress-making.

'Well, it's certainly different,' admitted Kiki, her eyes dancing with mirth.

The door to Bluebell Branch swung open, and

Mrs Hover, the matron, bobbed heavily into the room. 'I thought as much!' she said grimly when she caught sight of Sooze. 'Think again, my lovely.'

'Oh, but Hovey –' started Sooze, her eyes wide and innocent.

'Go on, now – I want a proper dress from you in two wing beats!' Mrs Hover shook her head as Sooze flew off, still twirling her feathery boa. 'Slits in the skirts at your age! Whatever next? Come along, girls, I've got your new timetables.'

Crowding around Mrs Hover with the others, Twink received a pink rose petal with her name on it. She scanned the silver writing eagerly.

Star Magic II (glamours continued); Advanced Creature Kindness II (medium-sized mammals and birds); Advanced Flower Power II (fields and forests); Weather Magic III (managing storm systems); Advanced Fairy Dust II (tricky transformations); Introduction to Mood Magic.

'Mood Magic – glimmery!' said Twink with satisfaction. The art of influencing a place's mood was advanced magic, and she had been looking forward to it for ages.

'And look, we've got three classes together,' said Bimi, peering over Twink's shoulder. She smiled. 'It's a good thing – you're going to be spending all your time on the Fledge field now, so I'd never see you otherwise!'

Twink bumped against her. 'Don't be silly; we'll see each other loads.'

But she couldn't hold back a grin at the reminder that she was the new Games Fairy, and it only grew wider when the Bluebell Branch fairies flew down the trunk for breakfast. The oak-leaf notice she'd put up was hanging outside the Great Branch, and there was a bright, jostling crowd of fairies hovering around it, talking excitedly.

FLEDGE TEAM TRY-OUTS
Would you like to be on the Fledge Team?
Are you a fast flyer?
Then come to the Fledge Field this afternoon –
Your Fledge Team needs you!
Twink Flutterby, Games Fairy

FLEDGE TEAM TRY-OUTS

Would you like to be
on the Fledge Team?
re you a fast fly ?
me to the Fl   ld
after
Te
Fl
s F

'Twink Flutterby, Games Fairy,' mused Sooze. She was now wearing a dress similar to Twink's, though the skirt was a bit shorter and flouncier. 'Mmm, that has a nice ring to it, doesn't it?'

Pix laughed as they fluttered into the Great Branch. 'Yes, Twink, I don't like to say we told you so, but –'

'But we told you so!' sang Sooze, linking her arm through Twink's.

'All right, all right,' laughed Twink. Her cheeks reddened as she saw that half the school was

watching her, whispering and smiling in admiration.

'Twink, congratulations!' squealed Teena, flitting over from the Daisy Branch table to give her a hug. 'Mum and Dad are going to be thrilled.'

'Thanks, Tee,' said Twink, returning the embrace. 'Do you know if Summer's trying out for the team?' Summer was a friend of Teena's, and excellent at sport.

Teena nodded vehemently. 'Of course! You couldn't keep her away.'

Other congratulations followed as Twink made her way to the Bluebell Branch table. Even Mariella gave her a smile as they sat down. 'Well done, Twink,' she said, tossing her silvery-green hair. 'Of course, *I* don't have time for Fledge any more, but if you can fit it into your schedule, then good for you.'

Twink held back a smile. She decided not to mention that the reason Mariella didn't have time for Fledge any more was because of her poor marks, which often meant she had to take extra lessons!

Suddenly Romi came up to their table, fluttering her pale blue wings and looking disapproving. 'I see

that you've scheduled the try-outs already. Don't you think it's a bit soon?'

Twink shook her head in surprise. 'No, I don't. I think the sooner the better, so that we can start practising.'

Romi raised an eyebrow. 'Well, I suppose you know best,' she said grudgingly, her tone implying the exact opposite. 'Anyway, I'll come along this afternoon and give you a hand, shall I?'

'That's really not necessary –' started Twink, but found that she was talking to thin air. Romi had already flapped away again.

Twink gaped after her, lost for words – and then she and Bimi looked at each other and burst out laughing. 'Oh dear,' said Bimi with a grin. '*Somebody's* got her wing out of joint!'

Chapter Three

Sixteen fairies showed up for the try-outs – including Summer, Twink was glad to see. The younger fairy skimmed up as Twink hovered on the edge of the Fledge field. Her orange hair was like a flaming sunset, and her smile just as bright.

'Hi, Twink – I can hardly wait to try out!' she said eagerly. And Twink knew it was true – she had taught Summer some Fledge moves a year ago now, and Summer had been longing to play for the school even then.

Twink wrote her name down with a smile. 'We're

just about to start. Why don't you go and warm up?'

Summer gave her a grin and a salute, and flew off on to the Fledge field – a circular patch of grass with a dozen posts rising out of it, each with a fairy-sized hole through the middle. The Flea sat preening himself on top of the tallest, centre post.

The rules of Fledge were simple: you were either trying to steal the Flea, or guard him. When you were Guarding there were only three of you, and you could tag the six Stealers as they swooped in, trying to grab the Flea. The game continued until either all six Stealers had been tagged, or the Flea had been stolen three times.

But of course the Flea never simply sat still during a game, thought Twink – he had a tendency to leap about wildly, with his Guards flying frantically after him! That was what made Fledge so exciting.

Organising the fairies into groups of four, Twink started them off with some practice moves. Just as she was settling down on the sidelines to watch and take notes, Romi raced up, red-faced and out of breath.

'You didn't wait for me! I told you I'd come and help,' she said crossly.

Twink pressed her lips together to hold back her irritated reply. 'Thanks, but I wanted to go ahead and get started,' she said. One of the teams *whooshed* past overhead, first turning barrel rolls in unison, and then separating to somersault through the poles.

Romi craned her head to read Twink's notes. 'You haven't said anything about Kym yet – she's a *brilliant* flyer, if you haven't noticed.'

'I've noticed,' said Twink, angling her petal pad away.

Romi tapped her wings together as she watched the fairies go through their paces. 'Maybe you should start them off with a practice game, instead of these moves,' she suggested. 'I think that would be a much better way of –'

Twink slapped her snail-trail pen down. 'Romi, why don't you go and catch the Flea and get him ready for some Stealer moves?'

Romi blinked. 'Catch the Flea? But –'

'Yes, that would be really helpful,' said Twink firmly. For a moment the purple-haired fairy hesitated, looking disgruntled – but finally she flew off on to the field after the Flea. Twink let out a relieved breath.

As the try-outs continued, it became clear to Twink that Summer was an even better player than she'd first thought. The second-year fairy sped about the field as if she'd been born to it. During the practice game she scored twice by stealing the Flea, and even managed to tag a Stealer when she was playing on the Guards' side.

Twink felt her pulse quicken as she watched. Summer was a natural! And a few of the other players were really good, too – particularly a green-haired fairy called Jacki, and the fairy called Kym who Romi had pointed out earlier.

When the try-outs were over, Twink called everyone around. They hovered in a circle, breathing hard from the workout.

'Thanks for coming, everybody,' said Twink sincerely. 'You've all played really well! I'll post the new team list in the Great Branch at dinner.' She was careful not to catch Summer's eye as the fairies flew back towards the school, but she knew already that she wanted the second-year fairy on her team.

'Well, what do you think?' demanded Romi the moment they were gone. '*I* think it's obvious – it has to be Jacki, doesn't it?'

Twink gritted her teeth as she put the Flea back in his cage. 'Actually, I'm going to put Summer on the team,' she said. 'Jacki and Kym will be our new reserves.'

'*Summer?*' Romi propped her hands on her hips.

33

'But she's only a Second Year!'

'And?' Scooping up the cage, Twink flew off towards the Creature Kindness log, where the Flea lived between games.

Romi sped after her. 'Second Years are reserves, not *players*. She's not experienced enough!'

'She'll be fine,' said Twink shortly, banking to avoid a spiderweb. 'She was the best player by far – why would I waste her as a reserve?'

Romi shook her head as they landed in front of the Creature Kindness log. 'OK, maybe she's good during a *practice,* but how will she be when the real pressure's on? You need to make sure she's got what it takes before you –'

Twink spun round to face her. 'Fine, I've got the idea! But Summer's going to be on the team, and that's all there is to it.'

Romi's voice was stiff. 'Well, I can see that I can't talk you out of it – but I think you're making a mistake, Twink.' She took off back towards the school in a flurry of wings.

'Oh, who asked *you*, anyway?' muttered Twink.

Banging angrily into the log, she returned the Flea to his pen. He seemed to smirk at her as he leapt away. Like most fleas, he was a contrary creature who enjoyed discord . . . and suddenly Twink had a sinking feeling that he was going to see a lot of it over the next few weeks!

'Mood Magic is a very powerful art,' said Miss Moonbeam from the front of her classroom. She was a tall, slender fairy with light blue hair, whose pale wings shimmered like moonlight on water.

'Through the right use of spells and thought, we fairies can make a place seem happy, sad, or any emotion in between. Why, we can even influence humans!' She swept her arms out in a dramatic gesture.

Twink sat on her mushroom seat, absently scribbling notes. Now that she was finally taking Mood Magic, she could hardly keep her mind on it – she was too busy thinking about her first team meeting, which was scheduled for later that afternoon. She had spent hours planning it the night before, and could hardly wait to tell the team her ideas for the upcoming season!

She smiled, remembering how thrilled Summer had been to learn that she was on the team. '*Thank you*,' the orange-haired fairy had gasped, shooting straight up in the air in her excitement. 'Oh, Twink, thank you, thank you! You won't regret it, I promise!'

'I know I won't,' Twink had told her with a grin. 'And there's no reason to thank me, Summer – you're a brilliant player, that's all.'

Jacki and Kym, the two reserves, had been pleased as well. In fact, Twink was certain that Glitterwings had an excellent team this year – why, they probably had a good chance to win the Fairy Finals! Excitement tickled at her scalp, imagining it.

If they could just beat Sparklelight Academy, that was. Twink tapped her snail-trail pen against her teeth as Miss Moonbeam continued her lecture. Glitterwings had to beat Sparklelight at least twice this season to play in the finals, and it wouldn't be easy – Sparklelight had one of the best teams in the league.

Miss Moonbeam

'Isn't that right, Twink?' said Miss Moonbeam's voice.

Twink started, looking up in alarm. The Mood Magic teacher raised an eyebrow, waiting. 'I – I'm sorry, Miss Moonbeam. I wasn't paying attention,' admitted Twink.

Laughter rippled across the branch as Miss Moonbeam winked at her. 'Yes, I know. I was just saying that daydreaming is one of the easiest moods to slip into. I take it you agree?'

Twink's pointed ears grew warm. 'Er . . . yes, I suppose I do.'

'Good! But let's try for an alert, interested mood instead,' said Miss Moonbeam. 'Now, please open your books to page . . .'

Twink managed to keep her mind on the class for the rest of the lesson, but the moment the magpie's call echoed through the school, she leapt up and grabbed her things. The team was meeting in the Fledge log soon, and she wanted to be there before the others arrived.

'See you later, Bimi,' she said quickly.

Bimi nodded, her eyes shining. 'Good luck, Twink. You'll be great!'

The wind whistled through her lavender wings as Twink raced down the trunk and then shot out into the spring sunshine. The Fledge log was used for team meetings, and was located on the edge of the playing field beside the changing log. To Twink's annoyance, Romi was already there when she entered it.

'Oh,' she said, fluttering to a halt. 'Hi, Romi.'

'Hi,' said Romi briskly. She was setting up a large oak leaf on an easel made of twigs. 'I thought we might need this to write on,' she said. 'You know, to demonstrate set plays and that sort of thing.'

What do you mean, 'we'? thought Twink indignantly. The fact that it was a good idea just made her feel even more irritated. 'Thanks,' she said, putting her petal bag down.

'No problem.' Romi took a seat on one of the bark benches and folded her wings behind her back.

At least she didn't look as if she planned to lead the meeting herself – Twink supposed she should be grateful for that! Some of the other team members started coming in then, and she put on a welcoming smile. 'Hi, Cassi. Hi, Summer.'

The orange-haired fairy was starry-eyed as she took in the Fledge log. 'So *this* is what it's like inside!' she breathed, sinking down on to a bench. 'I've often wondered.'

Twink laughed. 'It's only a room with a few benches in it, really,' she said. 'But I know what you mean. It's glimmery seeing it for the first time!'

Soon all the team was there, apart from Vera and Zayna. Twink glanced out of the window, wondering what was keeping them. She began to feel very self-conscious. The rest of the team was watching her expectantly, with Romi sitting right in the front row. From the look on her face, she wasn't at all surprised that things weren't going to plan!

Twink's cheeks heated at the thought. 'Er . . . let's just wait a few more minutes for Vera and Zayna,' she said, fiddling with a bit of chalk that Romi had brought to write with. 'I'm sure they won't be much longer.'

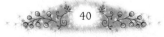

Romi jumped up. 'Shall I go and find them?'

'No, that's all right,' said Twink. 'They must be on their way.'

But the minutes crept by with no sign of them. Twink shifted awkwardly at the front of the log. Where *were* they?

Finally she cleared her throat. 'Um, Romi . . . maybe you'd better . . .'

Just then Vera and Zayna appeared, wafting in with lazy wing strokes. They were chattering away together, apparently not bothered by the time in the

least. 'Yes, and so then *I* said –' Vera broke off as she caught sight of Twink's expression. 'Oh, hi. We're not late, are we?'

'Just a bit,' said Twink weakly.

'Sorry!' said Vera with a bright smile. She didn't look particularly sorry, thought Twink. Nor did Zayna, for that matter.

Twink hesitated, wondering whether she should say something. But Vera and Zayna had taken seats beside Romi in the front row, folding their wings back and looking at her attentively, and she decided to let it pass.

'Right! I'd, um – like to welcome you all to our first team meeting of the new year,' said Twink. Her voice sounded unnaturally loud to her, but she kept on. 'I've got lots of new ideas for the team, and I'd just like to –'

Twink broke off. Romi's hand had shot into the air. 'Er . . . yes, Romi?'

'I know a glimmery set play we can do,' said Romi. 'I went to a special Fledge Camp over the hols, you know, and –'

'That's great,' interrupted Twink. 'But I just wanted to go over a few things first.'

'This won't take long,' said Romi. 'Then you can work the rest of your plans around it.' And without waiting for an answer, she leapt up from her bench and grabbed the chalk from Twink's hand.

Chapter Four

'It's called the Power Play,' said Romi, beginning to sketch on the oak leaf. 'See, usually when you're Guarding you're on the defensive, right? You're having to watch the Flea, and guard it from the Stealers. Well, with the Power Play, you make the *Stealers* go on the defensive! The three Guards all band together like this, and –'

Twink thought angrily that she might have known Romi's great idea would place the Guards in starring roles, since that was the position she herself played! She snatched the chalk back

from her. 'Thanks, but I don't think we'll be doing that.'

The team grew very quiet, watching the scene. 'But why not?' burst out Romi. 'It's a brilliant set play!'

'Because I've got other ideas in mind,' said Twink. 'Maybe we'll look at yours later.'

Romi sat down again crossly. Trying to smile, Twink quickly brushed away Romi's sketch. 'Right, where was I?'

The meeting fell a bit flat after that. Twink described her own plans, drawing on the leaf, and although the team seemed interested, she couldn't shake the feeling that they were all thinking about Romi's Power Play. *Why* couldn't Romi have spoken to Twink in private about her idea, instead of just taking over?

Gritting her teeth, Twink tried to push Romi out of her mind – which wasn't easy when the purple-haired fairy was sitting right in front of her, scowling!

'So, um, those are some of my plans,' concluded

Twink at last. 'Now, you all know that we've got to beat Sparklelight at least twice this season if we're going to make the Fairy Finals. So I'd like to schedule three practices a week, on Mondays, Wednesdays, and –'

'*Three?*' echoed Vera. 'We only ever had two with Madge!'

'I know,' said Twink. 'But we've got a lot of new players now, and –'

'Twink, I'm sure that I speak for all of us older girls when I say that we just don't have time for that,' said Vera firmly. 'We've got our Acorn Exams coming up, you know.'

'Yes, and I'll have my Sapling Exams this year,' pointed out Twink. 'But I still think it's important that we . . .' She trailed off. Zayna and Vera sat side by side, shaking their heads. The rest of the team looked undecided, glancing from Twink to Vera and back again.

Twink bit her lip. 'Well . . . what do the rest of you think?'

'*I* think two is plenty,' said Zayna immediately.

Cassi and Kym chorused agreement. Romi sat silently, gazing up at the ceiling with a knowing expression.

'I'm happy with three,' said Summer shyly. 'I think you're right, Twink – we have a lot of new players, and we need the practice.'

To Twink's dismay, Summer was the only one on her side. She swallowed hard, wondering if she ought to put her wing down and insist on three practices a week. But she didn't want to come on too strongly at first – the others might think that being the Games Fairy had gone straight to her head!

'All right,' she said finally. 'Let's – let's start with two practices a week, and see how we get on.'

'Brilliant!' said Vera, bouncing up from her seat. 'Well done, Twink – that was a really good meeting. See you on Wednesday, everyone!' And with that, she and Zayna flitted from the room, laughing and talking.

But I haven't ended the meeting yet, thought Twink, her wings drooping.

It appeared that it was over, though. The other team members started leaving as well, smiling their goodbyes to her. To hide her burning cheeks, Twink fussed over the oak leaf and easel, putting them away.

'Yeah, a really good meeting,' said a dry voice.

Twink looked up to see Romi beside her, shaking her head. 'You've got to be a lot firmer than that with *those* two, Twink,' she said in disgust. 'They like Fledge, but they don't like to work hard. They'll fly all over you if you're not careful!'

'I was firm,' protested Twink. 'I just asked

everyone what they thought, that's all.'

'Well, *I* think you're asking for trouble,' said Romi heatedly. 'But then, you're the Games Fairy, not me.' Her tone made it clear how unfair she thought this was. Without waiting for a reply, Romi jetted from the room.

Slowly, Twink gathered up her things and followed. *Never mind what Romi thinks,* she told herself as she closed up the log. *I want everyone to like me before I start throwing orders around! Besides, two practices a week are probably plenty.*

Even so, Twink's wings felt heavy as she flew back towards the school. Somehow being the Games Fairy seemed much harder than she had thought.

It didn't become any easier over the next few weeks. Vera and Zayna quickly made a habit of arriving late to practices, and then didn't seem to take them very seriously once they got there. More than once Twink saw the two of them hovering side by side on the Fledge field, chattering away while

49

the others practised their moves.

When Twink tried to talk to Vera about it, the older fairy blinked in surprise. 'But Twink, Zayna and I have been playing for years! We *know* all these moves already.'

Something in her tone made Twink feel like a beginner at the game. It was true that she hadn't been playing nearly as long as Vera.

She took a deep breath. 'Yes, but it's not just about knowing the moves yourself – it's about working with the other team members so that you all play together smoothly. We've got the Sparklelight game coming up next week, and –'

Vera laughed and patted her shoulder. 'We'll be fine! Don't worry, Twink. We'll beat Sparklelight, no problem.'

She flitted off, and Twink was left staring after her, biting her lip. Vera seemed so confident that suddenly Twink felt unsure of herself. Perhaps Vera was right, and she was worrying needlessly. Meanwhile, she supposed it wasn't harming anything to let Vera and Zayna have a bit of fun.

But as the days went on, the situation worsened. Some of the other fairies started to become affected by Vera and Zayna as well, so that practice times were rapidly becoming a time for jokes and merriment, rather than getting down to work.

Twink did her best to keep order, but it was difficult. If she didn't laugh along with the others then it would seem like she didn't have a sense of humour . . . and besides, some of the quips really *were* funny. *Maybe I'm just taking it all too seriously,* she fretted. Surely the team would calm down soon . . . wouldn't they?

None of this was helped by Romi's glowering presence. She did everything Twink asked of her, but with a look on her face that said that *she* would be doing a much better job as Games Fairy. The final straw came when Twink flew on to the field early one afternoon, and found Romi already there, teaching her Power Play to Cassi and Kym.

'You need to link arms and fly together,' she was saying as Twink flew up. 'No, not quite so tightly . . . yes, that's it. Good!'

'Romi, what are you doing?' demanded Twink. Cassi and Kym stopped mid-move, their eyes wide.

Romi crossed her arms over her chest. 'I'm *trying* to help the team, that's what.'

'Kym, you and Cassi go and practise your high-speed barrel rolls,' ordered Twink.

When the two fairies had sped off, she whirled towards Romi. The pent-up worries of the last few weeks all seemed to come together at once, and the words burst out of her.

'How dare you!' she cried. 'I *told* you we weren't going to use that play – and now you're going behind my back with it.'

'Well, you wouldn't listen to me!' retorted Romi. 'I thought I'd use the play during the Sparklelight game, and show you how glimmery it is.'

Anger sizzled through Twink. 'Oh, you thought *you*'d use the play, did you? So you were going to ignore my coaching, and just do whatever you wanted!'

'Why not?' snapped Romi. 'That's what Vera and Zayna are doing, and *they* get away with it. Besides,

somebody has to do something, or else we're going to lose the game!'

'What do you mean?' asked Twink sharply.

Romi huffed out a breath. 'I *mean*, you're not exactly holding it together, are you, Twink? Vera and Zayna are larking about, team members are coming late to practice – it's a shambles. A good Games Fairy knows when she needs help! Maybe you just haven't got what it takes.'

Twink felt herself go icy-cold. Though part of her knew that there was a lot of sense in what Romi had said, the older fairy's superior tone made it impossible for Twink to admit it. She thought she'd rather die first!

'I do *not* need help,' she hissed, clenching her hands into fists. 'And Romi, if you're so unhappy with how I'm managing the team, then you don't have to stick around, you know. In fact, I wish you wouldn't!'

Romi's face turned poppy-red. 'Fine!' she cried, her voice shaking. 'I *will* leave – but you'll be begging me to come back soon. And if Madge could see what you've done with her team, she'd be furious!'

Romi shot away towards the school. Turning round, Twink saw to her embarrassment that the rest of the team had arrived and were hovering nearby, watching. Summer bit her lip, looking worried.

Vera flew over and put an arm round Twink. 'Don't worry,' she said. 'There can only be *one* Games Fairy, and Romi has had a thorn under her wing for weeks now that it's not her. We're better off without her!'

And though Twink hoped fervently that this was true . . . she knew that she'd feel a lot better if, deep down, she didn't think Romi had been right.

Chapter
Five

The day of the first Sparklelight game dawned bright and sunny. As the rest of Bluebell Branch slumbered, Twink stood at her window and gazed down at the Fledge field, wondering what the game was going to be like. Jacki was playing in Romi's place, and though she wasn't a bad player, she wasn't nearly as good as Romi. And Vera and Zayna were being just as difficult as ever.

It's going to be a disaster, thought Twink glumly.

There was a soft movement from the next bed, and then Bimi appeared at her side. 'It'll all be fine,'

she whispered, slipping her arm through Twink's.

Twink let out a breath. 'Oh, Bimi, I hope so. But – but it just hasn't been easy so far, being the Games Fairy.'

She had told her best friend some of the problems she'd been having, and now Bimi gave her a little shake. 'Twink, don't let what Romi said get to you! You *do* have what it takes, I'm certain of it.'

Twink slumped her chin on to her hand. 'So how come it all feels like it's going so wrong?'

'You just need time to find your best wing stroke, that's all,' soothed Bimi. 'You've only been doing it for a few weeks – why, I bet even Madge wasn't perfect at first!'

Twink sighed. 'Maybe.' Straightening up, she squeezed her best friend's arm. 'Thanks, Bimi. Will you be at the game this afternoon?'

'Try and stop me!' laughed Bimi.

As Twink skimmed on to the Fledge field later that day to meet the Sparklelight Games Fairy, she saw that most of the school had turned out for the

game. The grandstand – made up of hundreds of tall mushrooms – was almost completely filled, packed with excited fairies looking forward to the first game of the year. 'GO GLITTERWINGS!' sparkled several fairy-dust banners.

Twink gulped as she flitted to a stop. She was used to playing in front of crowds, but not when *she* was the one in charge of the team. How on earth could she play well today, with everyone watching her every move? For a moment she was tempted to put Kym in the game as well, and coach from the sidelines!

The Sparklelight Games Fairy was a tall silvery-haired girl named Tasha. She gave Twink a friendly smile as she joined her on the field. 'Congratulations, Twink! I'd heard you were the new Games Fairy – that's really glimmery.'

'Thanks,' said Twink, trying to smile. If Tasha only knew all the difficulties she'd been having! The older fairy gave her a curious look, but there wasn't time to talk. Their two teams were hovering on the sidelines, waiting to begin.

Visiting players always brought their own Flea, and now Tasha held up the cage. 'Well, shall we get started? I think the Flea's getting restless.'

Twink nodded, and drew the casting pebbles from her pocket. The pebbles each had a white side and a black side, and whichever Games Fairy called the right colour got to choose whether her team would Guard or Steal.

'Is that a new Flea?' asked Twink. The hairy little insect had bright orange spots on his legs, and was bouncing up and down like he could hardly wait to get started.

Tasha nodded with a grin. 'We just got him a few days ago. He's a tricky one – you'll have to watch out!'

Twink won the casting, to enthusiastic cheers from the crowd. 'We'll be Stealers first,' she said promptly. Fledge was played for the best of two out of three matches, and being on the Stealer side was seen as having the advantage.

Tasha shrugged good-naturedly. 'Two minutes,' she said, flying off to her team.

Twink swooped over to where her own team was gathered. Poor Jacki looked terrified! Summer seemed nervous, too, though she managed a shaky smile as Twink flew up.

'Right, everyone,' said Twink. 'They've got a new Flea, so they're not really used to him yet. Keep your eye on that Flea! Don't let him out of your sight for a moment.'

The new players were watching Twink intently, nodding as she spoke. Vera and Zayna just looked amused. 'Oh, Twink, we know how to play!' said Vera with a confident laugh.

Twink bit back her response. 'They've got a new fairy playing Guard as well,' she continued. 'That girl with the short blue hair. Summer, I want you and Cassi to keep an eye on her especially.'

'Ooh, and what are the rest of us meant to do?' giggled Zayna.

Taking it seriously would be nice! thought Twink crossly. But before she could say anything, the school magpie gave his call, signalling that the game was about to begin.

Twink took a deep breath. 'Come on, everyone. Let's show them what we've got!'

She took off with her team in a rush of wings. The two opposing sides gathered on the field, the Sparklelight Guards taking up their positions around the centre pole. Their Flea sat atop it, poised to spring.

Twink hovered with the other Stealers. To her relief, Vera and Zayna looked ready for action now. They were both good players, she reminded herself. Perhaps she'd been unreasonable to expect them to pay more attention during practice.

The magpie shrieked again, starting the game. Instantly, the Flea bounded off the centre pole, right over the Guards' heads. They jetted after him, but he was practically a blur as he leapt about the field.

Twink motioned quickly to Summer, who whizzed around a pole to block the Flea's path. The insect promptly bounded off again, straight towards Vera – but Vera hadn't noticed Summer's move, and was slow to react. The Flea soared past her.

Twink grimaced. That should have been easy!

The same thing kept happening again and again as the game went on. Vera and Zayna were trying their best, but they were both rusty, and not used to playing with the new team members. Soon the crowd was groaning in frustration at a series of near misses.

Even so, the Sparklelight team was coming off worse – their Flea was like a mad thing! The Guards had to spend their time desperately chasing after him, rather than tagging Stealers. As a result, Glitterwings managed to catch the Flea three times, winning the first match almost despite themselves.

But when the teams switched sides, Sparklelight suddenly had the advantage. Twink's cheeks burned as she watched her three Guards – Vera, Zayna and Jacki – lose the Flea time and again. The Sparklelight Stealers moved together like dancers. It took them no time at all to capture the Flea three times and win the second match.

The final game was like a repeat of the first – except that Sparklelight was getting better at working with their Flea! By the time the Glitterwings team had caught him twice, the Sparklelight Guards had tagged four Glitterwings players, leaving only Twink and Zayna.

The Flea perched on top of a post, twitching his feelers. Twink started towards him, and then all at once Tasha flew out of nowhere. No! Twink hurriedly dived through the hole in the post.

'Oof!' grunted Tasha as she narrowly missed flying into it. The Flea waggled his tongue at her and then bounded off again, heading straight for Zayna as she zoomed away from a Guard.

Zayna didn't even see him. Twink winced as she

and the Flea crashed into each other. Recovering herself quickly, Zayna just managed to snatch the insect from the air. 'Got him!' she cried, holding him up.

The crowd cheered wildly, waving their banners and clapping their wings. Twink shook her head in a daze. Glitterwings had somehow won their first game of the year . . . but it certainly hadn't been through playing well!

After the game, the Glitterwings team hosted a small party for the Sparklelight players in the Glitterwings guest branch. Though Twink put a smile on her face as the two teams mingled and chatted, her heart wasn't in it. *What* was she going to do? She had to get her team into shape before their next game, but she had no idea how!

Tasha came up, sipping fizzy nectar from an acorn cup. 'Good game, Twink,' she said cheerfully. 'But you'll have to watch out for us next time, once we're more used to our Flea!'

Twink grimaced. 'Yes, I know. In fact, I'm not

really sure how we won *this* game.'

'Well, you certainly had a bit of luck,' admitted Tasha with a smile. 'What's up, Twink? Glitterwings usually has such a great team.'

Somehow, Twink found herself telling Tasha about the troubles she'd been having – how superior Vera seemed whenever she tried to talk to her, and how the fairies had been playing up during practices.

'I *knew* we needed more than two practices a week,' finished Twink. 'But everyone really hated the idea, so . . .' She trailed off.

Tasha had been listening sympathetically. 'I suppose it can't be easy for you, being younger than half your players,' she said. 'But Twink, you've really got to take control. You're not there to be their friend, you're there to be their leader! Who cares if they moan a bit? They'll soon get used to it.'

The chatter in the branch seemed to fade as Twink stared at her. 'You – you're right,' she said slowly. 'I've been so scared that the team won't like me that I haven't dared to put my wing down.'

Tasha gave her a friendly nudge. 'Well, don't be scared any more,' she said. 'You're a great player, Twink, and I bet you could be a good Games Fairy.' She grinned. 'Mind you, I don't know why I'm telling you all this. It just means you'll probably beat us at our *next* game, too!'

Tasha flitted off to talk to one of her players, and Twink munched thoughtfully on a piece of honey cake, turning the words over in her mind. Suddenly she realised that Tasha's advice had been exactly the same as Romi's . . . though Tasha was so nice that it had sounded very different!

Twink felt an unexpected pang as she glanced around her at the party. Romi should be here with us, she thought. Maybe the purple-haired fairy was prickly sometimes, but she was an excellent player – one of the best Guards they'd ever had.

Then Twink remembered Romi's scornful tone, and her wings stiffened. Well, good Guard or not, *she* certainly wouldn't be asking Romi back on to the team. It was difficult enough being Games Fairy without having Romi there, sneering at her every move.

Things were about to change, though. Twink glanced over at Vera and Zayna, laughing together by the window, and her jaw tightened firmly. Tasha was right. She was going to get her team under control . . . whether they liked it or not!

Chapter Six

The next morning Twink hung another oak-leaf notice outside the Great Branch, pounding the thistle-nail grimly into the wall.

**FLEDGE TEAM MEETING
TODAY AFTER LESSONS
IMPORTANT – BE ON TIME!**
Twink Flutterby, Games Fairy

A group of sixth-year fairies were heading towards the Great Branch for breakfast. Vera was with them, and she flew across to Twink. 'What's up?' she asked in surprise. 'I'm busy this afternoon; I've got to revise my Advanced Spellwork.'

Twink whirled around, scowling. 'Just be there!'

Vera's eyes widened. 'But –'

'I mean it, Vera,' snapped Twink. 'I expect to see you there, and that's that.'

She sped away before Vera could reply. Though Twink's heart was pounding, it had been a lot easier than she'd thought to be firm with Vera . . . in fact, after weeks of biting her tongue, it had been a relief!

Bimi had saved Twink a seat at the Bluebell Branch table. Her pretty face looked troubled when Twink told her what had happened.

'What's wrong?' asked Twink. 'Don't you think I was right to stand up to her?'

'Of course!' said Bimi quickly, fluttering her gold and silver wings. 'It's just . . . well, I don't know. Be careful, Twink. Maybe you've been too easy on them, but you don't want to go too far in the other direction either.'

Twink made a face. That was easy for *Bimi* to say,

she thought as she poured herself a cup of morning dew. She wasn't the Games Fairy, and didn't realise how difficult it had been. Well, Twink had had enough of feeling bossed around by her own team. She was going to take charge!

When the time for the meeting came that afternoon, Twink stood at the front of the Fledge log, tapping her lavender wings together. The team arrived in twos and threes, laughing and chatting . . . but as each group came through the door, they caught sight of her glowering expression and fell abruptly silent.

Soon everyone was there except for Vera and Zayna. Without a word, Twink flew to the door and locked it. The team stared at her in amazement.

'I've got a few things to say,' announced Twink, flitting to the front of the log. 'The first one is that –'

A rattling sound interrupted her as the doorknob moved back and forth. Vera and Zayna had arrived.

Twink sped back to the door and swung it open. 'You're late,' she informed them coldly.

Vera gaped at her. 'But I told you, I had things to do. I got here as quickly as –'

'That's enough!' yelled Twink. Vera gulped. Behind her, Twink heard absolute silence from the others. 'Being late isn't good enough any more,' she went on in a low voice. 'If you're late again, you're off the team. Is that clear?'

Vera had turned pale. 'But you can't –'

'Can't what?' Twink put her hands on her hips. 'Or did you think I wouldn't throw you off the team, just because you nominated me for Games Fairy? Well, think again, Vera!'

'But Twink, we were only a few minutes late,' protested Zayna. 'It's nothing to get your wings in a twist about –'

Twink swung towards her. 'And I've had about all I can take from you, too! The two of you are going to fly straight from now on, or you're *both* off the team – is that clear?'

The log was so quiet that you could have heard an ant sneeze. Vera and Zayna stared at Twink in a daze. Slowly, they nodded their heads.

A rush of triumph swept through Twink. 'Good!' she barked. 'Then take a seat and listen to what I've got to say.'

She flew back to the front of the room and faced the others. 'Now then,' she said. 'The way we played yesterday was *awful*, do you hear me? I will *not* put up with that sort of performance again.'

The fairies bit their lips, not looking at each other.

'But we won the game!' objected Zayna.

'Only because the Sparklelight team was even more rubbish than we were,' snapped Twink. 'And *they* had an excuse. What's your excuse, Zayna? Do

you think you were playing your best when you crashed into the Flea without even seeing him?'

Zayna's cheeks reddened. She stared down at her pixie boots without replying.

'Does anyone else have a comment?' demanded Twink, scanning the room. She felt a slight pang as she caught sight of Summer's stricken expression, but hardened herself and continued.

'Right. Well, we've tried two practices a week, but it's not working. So until I say otherwise, we're going to have four.'

'*Four?*' gasped Vera. 'But –' She broke off as Twink glared at her.

'Four,' repeated Twink grimly. 'And there will be *no* whispering, *no* laughing, and *no* larking about. Has everybody got that?'

No one moved.

'*Has everybody got that?*' shouted Twink, her words echoing through the log.

The team started in alarm. There were a few mumbled yesses and nods of heads. One or two of the fairies looked close to tears.

'Good!' said Twink. 'I'll post the new practice schedule tonight. And I'll expect you all back here tomorrow afternoon, on time and ready to work for a change. Meeting adjourned!'

The next two weeks of practice were very different than the beginning of term. The team arrived at the Fledge field promptly, and did whatever Twink told them without complaint . . . at least to her face. Twink suspected that they had quite a bit to say about her behind her back, but told herself that she didn't care. Tasha was right – she wasn't there to be their friend. The important thing was getting her team into shape!

As the weeks passed, the Glitterwings team improved by leaps and bounds. Vera and Zayna were both good players when they worked, and soon they were flying seamlessly with the others, performing tricky moves and set plays. And, now that they were no longer disrupting things, the rest of the team was playing well, too.

Seeing how much better everyone did when she

was firm, Twink was determined not to let up for a moment. 'Do you call that flying?' she yelled as Cassi and Jacki whizzed past after the Flea. 'Come on, you two – faster!'

They didn't respond, but Twink saw Cassi's jaw tighten as she put on another burst of speed.

Good, Twink started to say – and then held back. If Cassi was working hard, it was no more than she should have been doing all along. The same was true for all of them, except for Summer. The orange-haired fairy had taken practices seriously from the start.

Though Twink took satisfaction in how much better her team was performing, it was a lonely sort of feeling. Practices had become somewhat grim times, with none of the laughter of before. Her team hardly spoke to her. In fact, Twink realised with a jolt, half of them seemed *afraid* of her.

It was true that she shouted a lot these days, but what else could she do? They'd fly all over her if she didn't keep on top of them! Still, the realisation bothered Twink. It made her feel uncomfortable, in a hot, prickly sort of way . . . and that just made her shout even more.

As the second Sparklelight game approached, Twink felt the tension mounting within her. Somehow, it seemed very important that she could show Tasha how much the Glitterwings team had improved. But her players didn't seem to be concentrating now as much as they had been, and made silly mistakes that caused Twink to grit her teeth.

'Summer, what are you *thinking?*' yelled Twink at the final practice before the game. The orange-haired fairy halted mid-flight and swallowed hard. The other players hovered too, watching Twink with sullen expressions.

Twink flew up to Summer, still fuming. 'You let the Flea go right past you!'

Summer's cheeks reddened, clashing with her sunset-coloured hair. 'I'm sorry,' she said. 'I didn't see him.'

'You weren't looking, you mean!' Twink heard the angry tone in her voice, and stopped. Summer was

one of her best players, and she knew the error hadn't been deliberate. But she couldn't just let it go, or the others would think she was going soft.

'Five laps around the field,' she ordered. 'Don't let it happen again.'

Summer took off without a word, circling the field.

'Oh, I like that,' muttered a voice behind Twink. 'First she works us until we're ready to drop, and then we get punished when we're so tired that we make mistakes!'

Twink spun round. The team regarded her warily

as she stared at them, trying to work out who had spoken. It could have been anyone, she realised. None of them liked her any more.

I don't care, thought Twink stiffly. Still, maybe she *had* been working them too hard. She motioned towards the changing log. 'Practice over, everyone. Be ready to leave for Sparklelight after breakfast tomorrow.'

The team jetted off without a word. Summer, finishing her laps, headed for the log as well, not looking at Twink as she flew past.

Twink hesitated. Part of her wanted to follow Summer and apologise, but she held back. *I'm not here to be their friend,* she reminded herself. No one had said that being the Games Fairy would be easy, had they?

Feeling troubled, Twink turned away and flew back to Glitterwings.

'Go Sparklelight!' screamed the crowd, beating their wings together as one of their players whistled through the air after the Flea.

Sparklelight Academy was located behind a glistening waterfall in a leafy wood. Nearby, a circular pond served as the school's Fledge field, with the posts rising up out of the clear water.

Hovering above a lily pad on the sidelines, Twink watched with satisfaction as Vera, playing Guard, swooped in and tagged the Sparklelight player. Yes! Twink punched the air, fluttering upwards. A groan ran through the mushroom grandstand.

Glitterwings was playing well, there was no doubt about it – but so was Sparklelight. In the end, the home school took two of the three matches, winning the game, though each match had been so close that Twink couldn't feel bad about it.

'Well done!' said Tasha at the party afterwards. She tapped her acorn cup of fizzy dew against Twink's. 'Your team played brilliantly. I suppose things are going better for you, then?'

'Yes, lots,' said Twink. Her cheeks grew warm, and she quickly took a sip of dew. Things *were* going better . . . but only if you didn't count how her team felt about her!

The Sparklelight visitors' chamber was a cosy cave behind the waterfall. Sunlight flashed through the moving water, making dancing patterns of light on the walls. Twink had always loved this room, but now, caught up in her own thoughts, she hardly noticed it.

'What's up, Twink?' asked Tasha with friendly concern.

Twink managed a smile. 'Oh, nothing.'

Suddenly she wondered whether Tasha, too, found it difficult and lonely to be in charge. She opened her mouth to ask, but just then two of the Sparklelight players appeared, linking their arms through Tasha's with merry smiles.

'Come on, Games Fairy, we haven't had a chance to celebrate with you yet,' teased the Sparklelight Guard with short blue hair.

'Yes, we need our leader!' giggled the other fairy. With a resigned grin, Tasha said goodbye to Twink and allowed herself to be dragged over to her team. A moment later, they were all laughing together.

Twink couldn't help staring. She knew how firm

Tasha was with her players on the field, yet it was obvious that they loved her anyway. How on earth did she manage it?

Glancing over to where her own team stood talking together, Twink bit her lip. Slowly, she flew across the room. 'Good game, everyone,' she said as she landed beside them. 'I'm – I'm really proud of you.'

The Glitterwings players had stopped talking the moment Twink touched down. There were a few strained smiles, but no one responded. Summer was staring down at her pixie boots with a frown.

Twink fluttered her wings, trying to pretend that nothing was wrong. 'So now we only have one more Sparklelight game,' she said brightly. 'And if we win that one, we'll be in the Fairy Finals!'

'Yes, glimmery,' said Vera, not looking at her. The team murmured agreement, but no one's heart seemed in it.

Silence fell, until the only sounds were the rushing of the waterfall and the Sparklelight team laughing and talking. Twink swallowed. 'Well –

well, I'm going to go and get some more cake. More cake, anyone?'

'No, thanks,' muttered a few voices. Twink's wings felt hot as she flitted over to the refreshments table. From behind her, she could hear a sudden burst of whispered conversation.

They hated her. Twink blinked back tears. It was so unfair! Yes, she had been harsh with them, but only because she wanted them to play well. Didn't they realise that?

Picking listlessly at a bit of honey cake, Twink gazed at Tasha again. Despite her advice, the Sparklelight Games Fairy seemed to have found a way to be both her team's friend *and* their leader.

Twink's mouth tightened. Well, maybe that worked for Tasha, but it hadn't worked for her. When *she* had tried being nice, things had been a mess! If being stern was what she had to do to make her team perform well, then she'd do it.

But the thought wasn't a pleasant one, somehow . . . whether they got into the Fairy Finals or not.

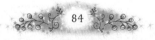

Chapter
Seven

'Twink, can I see you for a minute?' called a tentative voice.

Twink glanced up from her Mood Magic homework in surprise. Summer was hovering in the doorway of the Fourth Year Common Branch, looking ill at ease. Younger students didn't normally go to the common branches of older ones, and Twink saw several raised eyebrows on the fairies around her.

'Impudent thing!' grinned Sooze from the next mushroom desk as Twink got up. 'You wouldn't have caught *me* doing that at her age.'

'No, you were even younger!' laughed Sili from a few mushrooms away.

Fluttering to the doorway, Twink lowered her voice. 'Summer, what are you doing here?'

The orange-haired fairy shrugged, looking down. 'I need to talk to you, that's all.'

'Well – can't it wait until practice tomorrow?' asked Twink in bewilderment.

Summer shook her bright head. 'No. You see, I – I won't be at practice.'

'Won't be at practice!' Twink raised her voice without meaning to. Glancing over her shoulder, she drew Summer further out on to the ledge and shut the door behind them. 'Why not?'

Summer took a deep breath. 'Because – I'm quitting the team.'

It felt as if the ledge had fallen away from beneath Twink's feet. 'Quitting the team? But – but Summer, *why*? You're one of our best players!'

Summer shifted uncomfortably. 'I just . . . don't want to play any more, that's all.'

'Is it because I shouted at you the other day?' pressed Twink. 'Look, I'm really sorry about that, but you can't leave the team because of it –'

'No, it's not because you shouted at me,' broke in Summer. 'It's . . . it's because all you ever *do* is shout now. It's just not fun any more, Twink. I'm sorry.'

A prickly anger swept over Twink. 'Well, it's not only about having *fun*, Summer,' she said heatedly. 'Playing well is a lot of hard work – that's what Fledge is all about!'

Summer's violet eyes looked sad. 'Is it, Twink?' she said softly.

She waited for a response, but Twink found herself staring at her, too dumbfounded to speak. After a moment, Summer turned and flew away down the trunk, growing smaller and smaller, until finally Twink lost sight of her altogether.

Back in the Fourth Year Common Branch, Twink stared glumly at her Mood Magic homework, hardly seeing the words on the page.

'Are you OK?' whispered Bimi, leaning over from the next mushroom. On Twink's other side, Sooze and Sili were busy studying together.

Forcing a smile, Twink nodded. She couldn't tell Bimi, not just yet. It was too humiliating!

Though Bimi looked doubtful, she turned back to her own work. Twink gazed downwards, playing with her snail-trail pen.

Though she tried to tell herself it didn't matter that Summer had quit, she knew it *did* matter. What sort of team was she running, when such a talented player as Summer didn't want to play on it?

Well, she couldn't do anything about it now. Twink sighed, forcing herself to concentrate on her Mood Magic homework. Then her pen slowed as she remembered their lesson earlier that day.

'Moods have a power of their own,' Miss Moonbeam had said, tapping her pale wings together. 'And managing your *own* mood is the start of performing mood magic. Let me show you.'

Drawing herself up to her full height, Miss Moonbeam had fallen silent as she regarded her class. She let the pause grow longer and longer, until the fairies shifted uneasily, wondering what she was doing.

Twink had winced as an unpleasant chill shuddered through her. Suddenly she realised it was coming from Miss Moonbeam. Their teacher's eyes had narrowed, and she was regarding them with an icy expression.

'I want you to get into pairs so we can practise,' she said. The class gulped. Though Miss Moonbeam's words were ordinary enough, the mood that was coming from her made it sound like a threat! They all scrambled to obey.

Then Miss Moonbeam smiled, and the tension drained away from the branch like snow in the sunshine. 'You see?' she said. 'Doesn't that feel very different than if I say *now*, "I want you to get into pairs?"'

Her students had stared at her in wonder. Pix's hand shot in the air. 'But Miss Moonbeam, how did you put on such an awful mood when it's not what you really felt?'

'Practice,' laughed their teacher. 'But you see how you must always be careful to notice what mood you're giving off. Your moods affect everything you do, so if you want something to be positive, then that's what your mood must be!'

As Twink recalled the scene now in the Common Branch, she suddenly felt as if icy water had been flung over her. What had *her* mood been like, these last few weeks?

I've been angry, she thought, rubbing her wings together. *And scared.*

But that wasn't all. Forcing herself to be honest, Twink realised there had been times when she'd actually *enjoyed* shouting at everyone and seeing them scurry to obey. It had been an angry sort of pleasure – the kind that twisted in your stomach like a snake – but pleasure nonetheless.

Suddenly Twink could hardly see her desk for the tears that had sprung to her eyes. How had this happened? All she had wanted was to be a good leader! No wonder everything with her team had gone so wrong. Maybe they were playing better, but

nobody was having fun any more . . . and it was all
because of her.

Romi was right, thought Twink dully. She *didn't*
have what it took to be a good Games Fairy. How
could she, when she had to be so horrid to get her
team to listen to her?

She thought back to when she had caught Romi
teaching her Power Play to Cassi and Kym. She had
been coaching them well, firmly and fairly, and they
had been listening to her. Just like Tasha's team
listened to her. And just like the Glitterwings team
had always listened to Madge.

Why, Romi was a lot like Madge, thought Twink suddenly. She didn't get on with everyone, because she had very definite ideas – but then, a good leader had to! You couldn't go around asking everyone's opinion, as Twink had tried to do at first.

I'm not enjoying this, realised Twink. Lost in thought, she doodled a Fledge field on her home-work paper. *I don't like what being the Games Fairy has done to me, or the team. I've turned into a bully, and – and I'm unhappy.*

Twink let out a shaky breath. Suddenly the way forward seemed very clear to her ... and it was a huge relief!

'Romi, could I talk to you?' called Twink.

It was the next morning before breakfast, and Twink was hovering to one side of the Great Branch as a rainbow stream of fairies flew past. Romi left her friends and flew over with a frown. 'What is it?'

'Would you come to a team meeting after lessons today?' blurted out Twink.

The purple-haired fairy folded her arms over her

chest. 'What for? I'm not on the team any more, remember?'

'Please, just be there,' urged Twink. 'It's important.' She held her breath, waiting.

Romi hesitated. 'All right,' she said finally. 'But, Twink –'

'Thanks, Romi!' broke in Twink with a grin. She flew quickly into the Great Branch before Romi could say anything else, feeling as if a weight had fallen from her wings.

Even so, when it came time for the meeting, Twink found it difficult to get the words out. Her team sat gazing at her in confusion, clearly wondering what was up. Romi perched to one side, not saying a word.

Twink cleared her throat. 'I've, um . . . asked you all to be here because I wanted to say a few things. The first is . . . I'm sorry.'

A surprised ripple passed through the team. Twink's cheeks reddened as she continued. 'You've probably heard that Summer's quit, and . . . well, I know it's all my fault. I've been horrid, always shouting and never saying anything nice to any of you. And – and that was really wrong of me, because you've been playing brilliantly these last few weeks!'

Her team stared at her in stunned silence. Twink swallowed hard. 'You see, I – I haven't found it very easy being the Games Fairy. I didn't know the best way to lead, and . . . I think I've made sort of a mess of it.'

Oh, she hadn't wanted to cry! But she could feel tears filling her eyes, and she swiped them away angrily.

'So that's why I've asked Romi to be here today,' she said. 'Because I think that she –'

Romi stood up. 'Twink's asked me to join the team again, and I've accepted,' she interrupted. 'And I'd like to say something, too. Twink, I shouldn't have been teaching the Power Play when you'd told me not to. It won't happen again.'

Twink's mouth dropped open. Romi stared back at her. *Go along with it!* her gaze said.

'Um . . . good,' faltered Twink, her thoughts

spinning. 'Well – welcome back to the team, Romi. There's not going to be a practice today, everyone,' she added quickly. 'You've all been working really hard, and – and I think three practices a week is probably plenty from now on. See you tomorrow.'

As her team flitted out, Vera and Zayna hung back, looking uncomfortable. 'Twink, we're sorry too,' burst out Vera. 'Zayna and I made things pretty tough for you at first, didn't we?'

Zayna nodded sheepishly. 'We just wanted to relax and have some fun, with Madge gone, but – but it wasn't very nice of us. We're really sorry.'

'That's OK,' murmured Twink in amazement. She stared after the two fairies as they left, and then slowly turned to Romi. 'Why did you do that?' she demanded.

Romi lifted a wing. 'You were going to quit, weren't you? And ask the others if they'd have me as Games Fairy instead.'

'Yes, and it would have been the right thing to do!' burst out Twink. 'I've been thinking, and I can see now that you were right. I – I just don't have what it takes.' Her throat felt sandy suddenly, and she looked away.

Taking her arm, Romi sat them both down on one of the bark benches. 'It *wouldn't* have been the right thing,' she insisted. 'I've been doing some thinking too, Twink. The team elected you, not me.'

Twink made a face. 'Yes, but only because Vera didn't want to have to work hard – you heard her just now!'

'Maybe,' said Romi, tapping her wings together. 'But they still elected you, and I think you could be brilliant, if you tried.'

'If I tried!' echoed Twink. She laughed in disbelief. 'All I've been *doing* is trying – nothing seems to work!'

Romi rolled her eyes. 'You've tried being some tough fairy, barking orders, and you've tried being so nice that everyone flies right over you. How about just being yourself for a change?'

Twink sat very still as Romi went on. 'You've got good instincts, Twink. You were right about Summer, for instance – she's a wonderful player! I

wouldn't have put her on the team, but you did.'

'Yes, and now she's quit,' said Twink gloomily. Propping her elbows on her knees, she slumped her chin on her hands.

Romi shook her arm. 'She'll come back if you ask her to, I know she will! And Twink . . . since everyone else is apologising, I suppose I should as well.'

Twink looked up in surprise as Romi's ears turned pink. 'I was a real moss brain to you, wasn't I? Acting like you couldn't do anything right, and always trying to take over. Well, I'm sorry. I told myself that it was for the good of the team, but – but I was just jealous that I wasn't the Games Fairy, that's all.'

Twink stared at her, feeling almost cross. 'So why won't you be the Games Fairy *now*, when I want you to be?'

Romi laughed as she pulled Twink to her feet. 'Because *you're* the Games Fairy, and I think you could be a great one. Just be yourself, Twink! What have you got to lose?'

Chapter
Eight

To Twink's surprise, her apology went a long way towards clearing the air with her players. During practices in the weeks after, the Glitterwings team listened attentively to her instructions, and performed even better than before.

It wasn't all smooth flying, of course. More than once, Twink had to mutter *just be myself* under her breath, as a reminder not to be too hard or too soft with them. But for the most part, the tension that had hung over the team like a dark cloud for weeks now had vanished – and little by little, Twink began

to feel more confident as a leader.

Her team seemed a lot happier, too. Although practice times were still mostly about working hard, there were also plenty of laughs. The difference was that her team respected her now, and would stop the jokes when she said so.

'Good one, Summer!' shouted Twink, clapping her hands as she hovered on the sidelines. Summer held up the Flea with a triumphant grin.

Thankfully, Summer hadn't taken much persuading to return to the team. And although Twink was delighted to have her back, she wasn't sorry that the orange-haired fairy had left in the first place. If she hadn't, Twink might never have realised what a moss brain she was being! She shuddered at the thought.

'Right, everyone, let's put the Flea away and get into pairs – I want to practise our high-speed pole manoeuvres,' called Twink. As they all got into position, Twink spotted Romi pairing up with Jacki.

Neither Romi nor Twink had said anything else about the Power Play. Half a dozen times now,

Twink had started to ask Romi to explain it to her . . . and half a dozen times she had firmly shut her mouth. Even though she was doing much better at being in charge these days, it felt important that she did it on her own. The Power Play was Romi's move, not Twink's. Using it would be like admitting that she still needed help.

The fairies zoomed about the field in pairs, their wings flashing as they shot through the poles. Twink noticed with satisfaction how much they had improved over the last few weeks. Sparklelight wouldn't know what had hit them!

'That's all,' called Twink when everyone was panting from the high-speed exercise. 'Good practice, you lot. Now, the final Sparklelight game is tomorrow, so I want you all to get a good night's rest. Remember, we almost beat them last time. We can do it!'

'Hi, Twink,' said Tasha as they met out on the Fledge field the next afternoon. 'Nice day, isn't it?'

'Yes, lovely,' laughed Twink. It was grey and misty,

with a damp chill in the air. 'Ready?' she said, taking out the casting stones. Her heart beat faster as she held them in her hand.

'White,' said Tasha.

Twink threw the three stones, holding her breath for them to land black side up . . . but they landed showing two white faces. A good-natured groan ran through the grandstand. The Glitterwings students were out in full force again, crowding the mushroom seats.

'Stealers,' said Tasha with a grin.

Twink nodded, trying not to show her disappointment. 'Two minutes.'

Once the match started, Twink could tell that Sparklelight had become used to their new Flea, and were often able to guess his next moves. The Glitterwings Guards did their best, but Sparklelight won the first match with a glimmery double-play, capturing the Flea before the Guards could tag their last two players.

The second match, with Glitterwings now playing on the Stealer side, went on for ages as the crowd watched breathlessly. The two teams were almost equal in skill, but Glitterwings were on their home field and had the Stealer advantage. Finally they took the second match with a flourish, as Summer jetted through a pole and snatched the Flea from under a Guard's nose.

'HURRAH!' screamed the crowd, fluttering up from their seats in a massive rush of wings. 'Go Glitterwings!' The fairy-dust banners waved brightly against the gloomy sky.

Even so, Twink frowned worriedly as the two teams changed sides for the final match. The fog was getting worse, and the Sparklelight flea was so difficult to guard! Twink didn't think they had a chance.

Romi's Power Play popped into her mind. Part of her wanted badly to ask the purple-haired fairy for help, but the words just wouldn't come. She had worked so hard to be a good Games Fairy . . . and now, whether her team won or not, Twink knew that the leadership had to come from her.

'Right, everyone,' she said, gathering them around

her. 'I want Romi, Vera and Cassi playing Guard –
and keep an eye on that Flea! One of you needs to
stay right with him at all times.'

Her players nodded grimly. 'Good luck!' said
Twink, and they flew back on to the field.

A light rain started. Twink saw that the crowd
were now using their banners to shield themselves
from the wet. On the field, it had become harder to
see than ever. The grey flea was almost invisible in
the misty rain.

Twink hovered on the sidelines, watching tensely
as the match progressed. It was just as she had
feared. Though Glitterwings was playing well,

Sparklelight was only two players down by the time they had stolen the Flea twice.

Twink grimaced as Romi dived at a Stealer and missed. Meanwhile, the Flea was leaping from pole to pole, with Cassi and Vera chasing after him in the drizzle. They were doing their best, but there were too many Stealers still left for them to keep an eye out in every direction.

We're going to lose, thought Twink in dismay. To her side, Summer and the others were watching the field as anxiously as she was. 'Come on, come on,' she heard Summer mutter.

Twink's jaw grew tight. Her team was looking to her for leadership, and she couldn't do anything!

On the field, Tasha started to fly towards the Flea. 'Watch it, Tash!' cried one of her players.

Glancing over her shoulder, Tasha neatly changed direction as Cassi swooped after her, missing her by a wing's breadth. 'Thanks!' she called to her teammate.

Twink stood very still as the realisation roared through her: Tasha was a brilliant Game Fairy – but she didn't do it all on her own. She took help when it was needed. Suddenly Twink found herself flying up into the air, waving her arms frantically.

'Time out!' she yelled. 'Time out!'

Each team was allowed two time outs during a game, and at Twink's shout the match stopped. Tasha's team hung about the field, chatting, as Twink's players gathered round her.

'What's up, Twink?' asked Romi, pushing back her damp hair.

'Romi, I want you to take over for the rest of the game,' said Twink.

The older fairy gaped at her. 'Take *over*?'

'Yes!' insisted Twink. 'You've got to teach us your Power Play – you're the only one who knows it.'

Romi looked taken aback. 'But –'

'But nothing,' interrupted Twink. 'Don't you remember what you said to me? A good Games Fairy knows when she needs help. Well, I need help – and I'm asking for it!'

The other players stared at Romi with hopeful expressions. Slowly, she smiled. 'All right, Games Fairy – I'll do it!'

She turned to address the team. 'Well, this move really needs a bit of practice, but I agree with Twink that it's our best chance. Twink, I want you, Summer and Zayna to take over as the Guards.'

'Us?' Twink blinked in surprise. 'But we're Stealers!'

'Yes, but it's more of a Stealer move than a Guard one. Now, what I want you to do is . . .'

Twink's wings began to tingle as Romi explained the play. She exchanged an eager glance with Summer and Zayna. The Power Play was an outrageous move — but if it worked, it was going to be brilliant!

The magpie's call sounded, signalling the end of the time out. Twink and the other two flew out on to the field. There was a startled buzz as the crowd saw that the players had changed.

The Flea sat on the centre post. Normally the Guards hovered loosely around him at the start of play, but now Twink and the others surrounded the little insect in a tight circle, not quite touching him.

The Sparklelight team had got into their places as

well. Tasha was frowning, obviously trying to work out what was going on. Twink grinned to herself. With any luck, she was about to find out!

The magpie's call sounded again, and the players fluttered into action. 'Now!' cried Twink.

Quick as light, Zayna grabbed the Flea and held him tightly against her chest. With their arms linked through hers on either side, the Glitterwings Guards flew straight at the Stealers.

Twink saw Tasha's eyes widen as she realised what they were doing. So long as Zayna was clutching the Flea, no Stealer could grab him without getting tagged by Summer or Twink – and meanwhile,

banded together, the three of them could go after whichever Stealer they liked!

'One . . . two . . . three . . .' counted Zayna as they shot across the field.

The rules of Fledge said that the Guards could only take hold of the Flea once per match, for up to thirty seconds. This was mainly so that the Guards could catch the insect if he went out of bounds – but, as Romi had pointed out, there was nothing in the rules that said they couldn't hold on to him for some other reason!

The remaining Sparklelight players jetted away in a frenzy, with the Guards right behind. Summer quickly tagged two of them, and then the trio turned neatly in the air, diving downwards so that Twink could snag a third.

'HURRAH!' screamed the crowd, bobbing up and down above the grandstand like excited bumblebees. Their banners waved in the rain.

'Seventeen . . . eighteen . . . nineteen . . .' chanted Zayna. She held tight to the Flea as he struggled sulkily.

'Hurry!' cried Twink. 'There's only Tasha left!'

The Sparklelight Games Fairy led them a merry chase, darting this way and that about the field. 'Twenty-one . . . twenty-two . . . twenty-three . . .' continued Zayna. The Flea writhed in her grasp, kicking its legs.

Twink spotted a flash of Tasha's silvery hair around a post, and tugged at Zayna and Summer. 'Go left!'

The three of them plunged sideways, hanging on to each other. With a quick somersault, Tasha shot through a hole.

Breaking away from Zayna, Twink flew after Tasha on her own, diving through the hole in pursuit. Tasha had flown straight up and then twisted off to one side, and the wind whistled through Twink's hair as she followed.

'Twenty-eight . . . *oh*!'

Up above, Twink saw that the Flea had escaped Zayna's grasp and was bounding from pole to pole, heading straight for Tasha. Eyes narrowed in concentration, Twink put on a burst of speed. She almost had her . . . almost . . . yes!

Twink tagged Tasha's foot just before the Sparklelight Games Fairy reached the Flea. 'HURRAH!' screamed the crowd. They erupted into deafening cheers, waving their banners.

'We won! We won!' shrieked Summer, tackling Twink in a mid-air hug. Zayna and the rest of the team followed, piling into Twink in a jubilant, screeching group. The fairies drifted to the ground, wings fluttering.

'Romi!' Twink threw her arms around the purple-haired fairy. 'Your Power Play was brilliant!'

Romi squeezed her back, bouncing up and down. 'So was that final move of yours. Oh, Twink, we're really going to the Fairy Finals!'

'What a sneaky manoeuvre!' laughed Tasha. Swooping over to them, she offered her wing to Twink. 'But you'd better watch out – *we* know it now, and we'll be using it next time.'

Romi grinned as Tasha flew off after her players to the visitors' changing log. 'Yes, that's the only problem with it – when you use it, you teach it to

the other team! But don't worry, Twink — I've got a few other tricks up my wing.'

'Good,' said Twink firmly, linking her arm through Romi's. 'I'll be counting on you.'

'And we'll be counting on *you*,' retorted Romi with a smile. 'You're a great Games Fairy, Twink — just like I knew you could be!'

'Three cheers for Twink,' cried Vera excitedly. 'Let's hear it for Twink!'

'Hip, hip, hooray!' shouted the team, clapping their wings together. 'Hip, hip, hooray!'

Twink's cheeks caught fire, but she lifted her head with a shy smile. She gazed at them all — at Summer, with her orange hair and shining eyes, and Romi looking flushed and happy, and at Vera and Zayna and all the rest of them — and her heart swelled.

'Thank you — all of you,' she said. 'You're the best team ever!'

'So are you sorry now that you didn't resign?' teased Bimi as they got ready for bed that night.

Twink smiled as she combed out her long pink

hair. Overhead, the bluebells that hung over her bed gleamed in the light of the glow-worm lanterns. 'Well, at first I wasn't sure,' she admitted. 'But Bimi, I think . . . I think maybe I might be a good Games Fairy after all.'

'Of course you are,' said Bimi warmly. 'I never doubted that you could be!'

With a contented sigh, Twink got up and gazed out of her window. The mist had cleared, and the Fledge field gleamed in the moonlight.

Twink thought about how excited she'd been when she was first made Games Fairy, though she hadn't really known anything about it – all she'd thought of was how important it sounded, and how exciting it would be.

Having so much responsibility had turned out to be very different from what she had thought . . . but Twink realised that she wouldn't change it for the world now, even knowing how hard it was. And that made it better, somehow – as though being Games Fairy really belonged to her, in a way that it hadn't before.

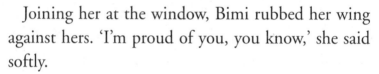

Joining her at the window, Bimi rubbed her wing against hers. 'I'm proud of you, you know,' she said softly.

Twink leaned against her. 'Thanks,' she said.

Further along their loft, Pix and Sili were going over their Flower Power homework together. Up above, Twink could hear Sooze's voice, arguing good-naturedly with Mariella. 'Now, look here, Mosquito-Nose . . .'

Propping her chin on her hands, Twink breathed in the smells of the damp spring night. How lucky

she was, to be a fourth-year student at Glitterwings Academy – and the school Games Fairy too!

The poles on the Fledge field rose up in the moonlight as Twink thought of all the games her team would play there over the next few years. And whether they won or lost, she would be there, doing her best to lead them.

'You know what, Bimi?' said Twink after a pause.

'What?' asked her best friend with a friendly nudge.

Twink smiled. 'I'm sort of proud of me, too.'

Turn over the page
and read the glimmery
beginning of Twink's
next adventure

From Fairy in Danger

Hurrah, we're back at Glitterwings Academy! Twink Flutterby smiled as she and her little sister Teena landed on the green, grassy lawn.

The giant oak tree that housed their school towered above them. The grand double doors at its base stood open, and arched windows spiralled up its trunk, sparkling brightly in the sunshine. Everywhere Twink looked, there were returning fairies. They swooped about calling to each other, or flew in and out of the school in a busy stream.

Twink sighed contentedly as she put down her oak-leaf bag. 'Glitterwings is *so* pretty in the summertime,' she said.

Teena laughed. 'You sound just like Mum!'

Twink grinned as she realised her little sister was right. Their mother had also gone to Glitterwings as a young fairy, and was always exclaiming over its beauty in every season.

'Well, it *is*, though,' insisted Twink. 'Look how green its leaves are!'

'You look – I'm going to go and find Zuzu,' said Teena, referring to her best friend. 'See you later, Twink!' She sped off towards the second-year section, her long pink hair and lavender wings looking very like Twink's own.

Twink stood where she was for a moment, still gazing upwards. Suddenly her violet eyes widened. What was *that*? There had been a flash of light at the top of the school, like a wink of fire!

Wings fluttering, Twink lifted up from the ground. She could just make out a slender branch growing right at the tree's peak. The light she'd seen was a window, catching the sun.

Twink stared at it in surprise. She'd been going to Glitterwings for over three years now, and she'd never known that there were any branches with windows that high up! What was the little branch used for?

Titania Woods

There are lots more stories about Glitterwings
Academy – make sure you haven't missed any of them!

If you have any difficulty in finding these in your local bookshop,
please visit www.bloomsbury.com or call 020 7440 2475
to order direct from Bloomsbury Publishing.

Visit www.glitterwingsacademy.co.uk for more fabulous fairy fun!